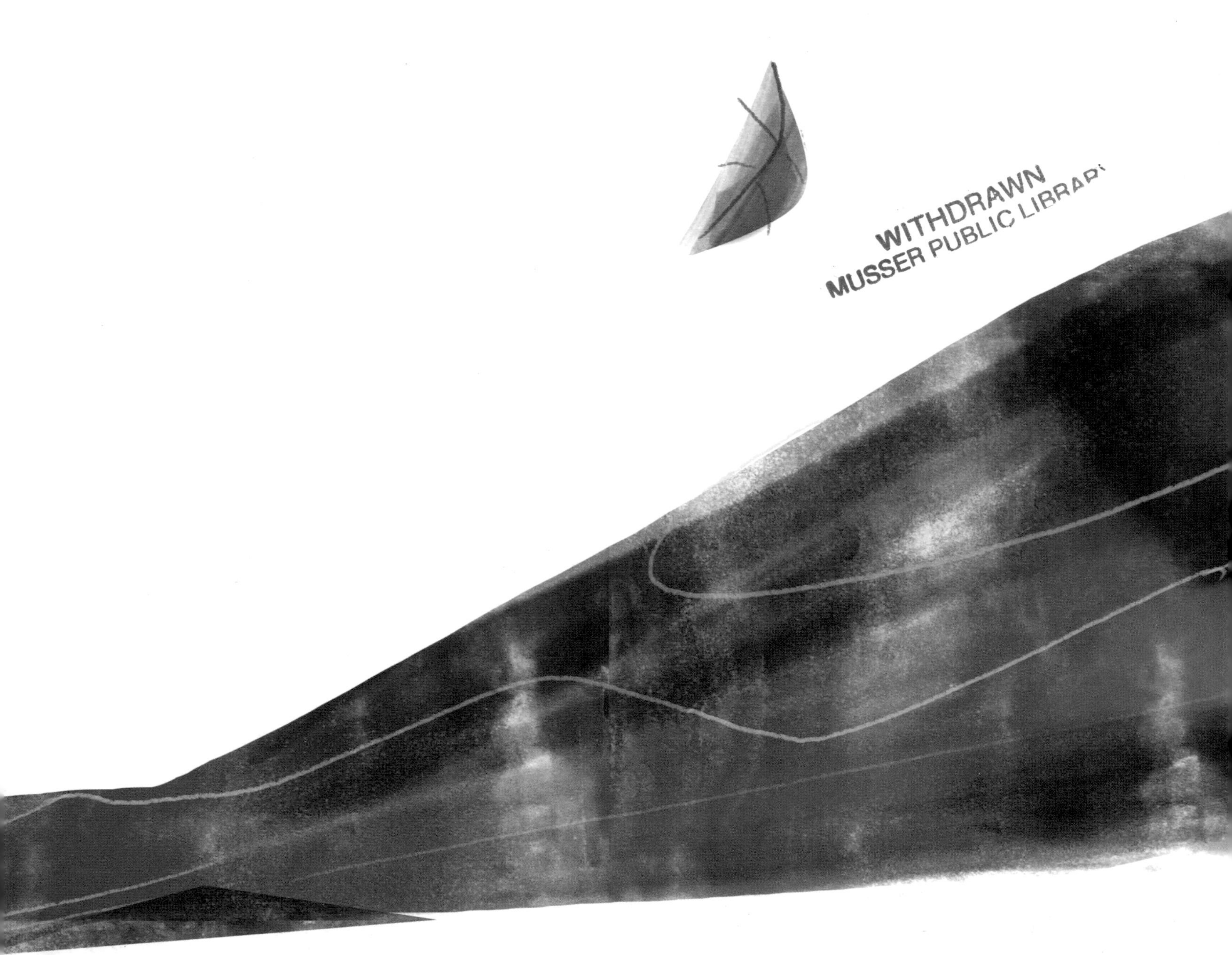

For Sage
—C.B.

For Eli (Sunshine) Jack, love Dad
—C.J.

Printed in Malaysia
First Edition, February 2016
1 3 5 7 9 10 8 6 4 2
FAC-029191-15288

Library of Congress Cataloging-in-Publication Data
Barton, Chris.
That's not bunny! / Chris Barton ; illustrated by Colin Jack.—First edition.
pages cm
Summary: A hungry hawk is outsmarted by the rabbit he hopes to have as a meal.
ISBN 978-1-4231-9086-8
[1. Hawks—Fiction. 2. Birds—Food—Fiction. 3. Rabbits—Fiction. 4. Humorous stories.] I. Jack, Colin, illustrator. II. Title. III. Title: That is not bunny!
PZ7.B2849Th 2016
[E]—dc23 2015000712

Designed by Tyler Nevins
Text is set in Appleberry
Art is created digitally using Adobe Photoshop

Visit www.DisneyBooks.com

That's Not BUNNY!

Words by
Chris Barton

Pictures by
Colin Jack

DISNEY • HYPERION
Los Angeles New York

From high in his perch, Hawk waited for his chance.

In the garden below, a movement caught his eye.

Down he sped,

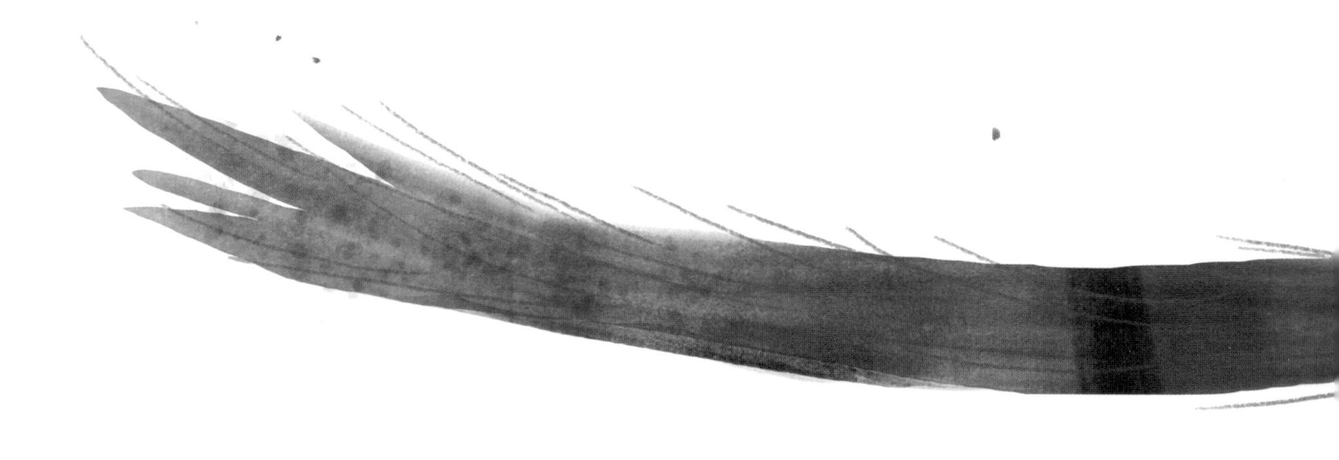

talons open,

beak poised,
to scream in victory.

SWOOS

And he screamed,
all right.

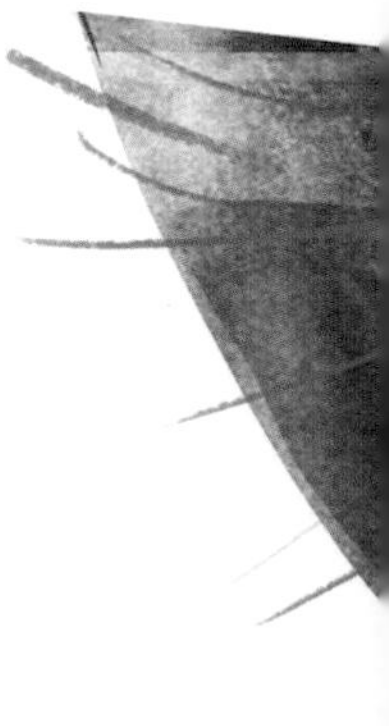

"A CARROT?!?"

He was so startled by his catch
that he just dropped it in his nest.

Hawk blinked a few times.

Now, was he a *carrot* hawk,

or was he a
hawk hawk?

He resolved to
try again.

Hawk perched.

He spotted.

Down he sped,
a fierce scream
at the ready.

SWOOSH

And he screamed,
all right.

"A CUCUMBER?!?"

Dismayed again, he
hid his bumpy green kill
in his nest.

Hawk shook his noble head.
Was he a *cucumber* hawk,
or was he a *hawk* hawk?

He set out
once more.

From his perch, he spied his prey and zeroed in.

Screaming remained an option.

And he screamed, all right.

"LETTUCE?!?"

"Oh, come on! I just hunted a HEAD OF LETTUCE?!?"

He landed with his prize, disgusted with himself.

He stomped and kicked and tore at the contents of his nest.

"I'm no *hawk* hawk!"

"I'm a carrot hawk.

I'm a cucumber hawk.

I'm a lettuce hawk.

I'm a...
I'm a..."

"Say..."

"Hi there," said Hawk.

"Hey," said Bunny.

"Want a salad?" asked Hawk.

"Sure," said Bunny. "What are you going to have?"

THE END